Dirty Bertie

JACKPOT!

DAVID ROBERTS WRITTEN BY **ALAN MACDONALD**

Stripes

Collect all the
Dirty Bertie books!

Contents

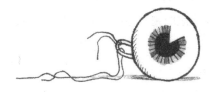

CHAPTER 1

Bertie thumped downstairs. The phone was ringing in the hall. Maybe it was Darren calling to say that school had burned down! He snatched up the receiver.

"Hello?"

"Hello, is that you, Bertie?"

"Oh hi, Gran, wassup?" said Bertie.

"You sound funny," said Gran.

Dirty Bertie

"Are you eating?"

"No, jush cleaning my teef," said Bertie.

"Well, never mind that, I've got some exciting news," said Gran. "You remember we stopped off at the supermarket on Wednesday?"

"Yes?"

"And you kept on and on until I bought a lottery ticket?"

"Yes?" said Bertie.

"Well, I WON!" whooped Gran. "We won! Can you believe it?"

Bertie thought he must be dreaming but no, he was wide awake with toothpaste dribbling down his jumper.

"REALLY?" he gasped.

"Yes really!" said Gran. "I've got the ticket right here. And anyway—"

"WAHOOOOO!"

Bertie dropped the phone, leaving Gran to talk to herself. He skidded into the kitchen where Mum and Suzy were having breakfast.

"WE WON! WE WON!" he yelled.

"Won what?" said Mum.

"The lottery!" shouted Bertie.

"Oh ha, ha," jeered Suzy. "We never do the lottery."

"No, but Gran did," said Bertie. "That was her on the phone. We actually won!"

Mum and Suzy stared at Bertie as if he'd lost his mind. They waited for him to burst out laughing and admit that it was a joke. But he didn't.

Dirty Bertie

"WE'RE RICH! WE'RE RICH!" he sang, bouncing around the room.

"What's all the noise?" asked Dad, coming in. "Shouldn't you be getting ready for school, Bertie?"

"Gran just phoned," said Mum. "She's got some news…"

"WE WON THE LOTTERY!" yelled Bertie.

Dad looked at him. "You're kidding!"

Bertie had to go over it all again. It was really him they ought to thank, he explained, because he'd talked Gran into buying a ticket. In fact, when you thought about it, half the money was his.

"How much will we get?" Bertie asked.

Dad sat down heavily. "I don't know, it could be millions," he said.

Dirty Bertie

"MILLIONS!" cried Bertie.

"What *exactly* did she say to you?" asked Mum.

"Nothing, just that we won the lottery," said Bertie.

They sat round the breakfast table, trying to take it in. Bertie's mind was already going into overdrive. Millions – think of that! He'd never actually seen a million pounds. Would the postman

bring it round in his sack? Or would it come on the back of a lorry? One thing was for sure, he was definitely going to need a bigger money box!

"I could give up work," said Dad in a daze.

"We could go on our dream holiday," said Mum.

"I could have my own pony," said Suzy. "Or even two."

"Don't forget it's *my* ticket that won," Bertie reminded them.

"Gran's ticket, you mean," said Mum. "And we shouldn't get carried away. She might not want to share the money."

Dirty Bertie

Bertie's face fell. Not share it? What would Gran do with a million pounds? She already got half-price travel on the bus! In any case, Gran was part of the family – she practically lived at their house! There was no way she'd keep a million pounds all to herself. He poured a second bowl of cereal.

"What are you doing?" asked Mum.

"Having breakfast," replied Bertie. "I can't go to school today, can I?"

"Too right you can," said Mum. "Now get a move on."

Bertie sighed. When he was a millionaire he definitely wasn't going to school. Spending all that money would be a full-time job. Wait till he told his friends – they would never believe it!

CHAPTER 2

Ten minutes later Bertie met Darren
and Eugene at the end of the road.
Mum had suggested they should keep
their lottery win a secret for now, but
Bertie wasn't very good at keeping
secrets. Besides, Darren and Eugene
were his best friends. He greeted them,
grinning from ear to ear.

15

"You're very happy for a school day," said Darren.

"Yes, I've had a bit of good news," said Bertie. "You'll never guess what."

"You've got peanut butter sandwiches," suggested Eugene.

"You actually finished your homework," said Darren.

"Much better than that," said Bertie. "We won the lottery!"

His friends stared at him in goggle-eyed amazement.

"The lottery?" said Eugene.

"You big liar!" snorted Darren.

Bertie just went on grinning at them. This was better than the time Miss Boot's chair broke when she sat down.

"It's true," said Bertie. "But it's a secret, so don't go blabbing it around."

Dirty Bertie

"You're serious?" said Darren. "How much?"

Bertie shrugged. "Dunno, probably millions."

"MILLIONS?" cried Eugene. "Woah! You'll be loaded!"

"We'll never have to walk to school again," said Darren. "We could go by helicopter!"

"I might give up school anyway," said Bertie breezily. "I can pay someone else to go for me – Know-All Nick for instance."

It wasn't a bad idea. He could hire Know-All Nick as his personal servant to carry his bag, clean his shoes and fetch important stuff – like ice cream.

Darren was thinking. "When do you get the money?" he asked.

"Pretty soon I expect," replied Bertie. "Gran's got the ticket."

Darren frowned. "Hang on, you mean it's not actually *your* ticket?" he said. "It's your gran's?"

"Well, yes," admitted Bertie. "But it was my idea, and anyway, I'm her favourite grandson."

Actually he was her *only* grandson – which was probably just as well.

£ $ ¥ € ₩

Bertie found it impossible to concentrate on lessons that morning. His attention always wandered when Miss Boot was talking, but today was worse than ever. All he could think about was one million lovely pounds. ONE MILLION! He could buy his own sweet shop,

Dirty Bertie

or a chocolate factory… He could live in a palace with a whole room for his bug collection…

"BERTIE!" bellowed Miss Boot. "GET ON WITH YOUR WORK!"

"Yes, Miss." Bertie sighed. The first thing he would do with his winnings was buy Miss Boot a one-way ticket to Australia.

CHAPTER 3

Back home, Bertie slammed the front door shut and threw down his bag. His mum was in the kitchen.

"Well, did it come?" he asked eagerly.

"Did what come?" said Mum.

"The money of course! The million pounds."

"It won't come here," said Mum.

Dirty Bertie

"It belongs to Gran. I've been trying to phone her all day but she's never in."

Bertie frowned. Surely Gran should be staying at home, in case the postman came.

"Anyway, I left a message," said Mum. "I said we'd take her out to celebrate tomorrow – at Dibbles' Tea Rooms."

Bertie raised his eyebrows. They never went out to tea and certainly not to Dibbles – the posh department store in town. Bertie thought that tea rooms sounded like the kind of place where people tutted when you burped. Still, there would be cakes and Gran could tell them all about their lottery win. Best of all, Dibbles had a toy department!

"Mum," said Bertie. "Can we go shopping tomorrow?"

Mum narrowed her eyes. "I thought you hated shopping," she said.

"Only clothes shopping," said Bertie. "But I think Dibbles has a toy department."

"I'm sure it does," said Mum. "But I'll need to talk to your father."

She thought it over. Normally she avoided taking Bertie shopping like the plague. He was forever picking things up, knocking them down or complaining that he wanted to go home. But maybe just this once. After all, if it wasn't for Bertie, Gran would never have won the lottery in the first place.

£ $ ¥ € ₩

The following afternoon, Bertie's family arrived at Dibbles department store.

Dirty Bertie

"Right, Suzy and I are off to look at shoes," said Mum.

"Wait a minute, what am I supposed to do?" grumbled Dad.

"You can look after Bertie," said Mum. "He wants to go to the toy department."

"Why can't you take him?" moaned Dad.

"I'm taking Suzy," said Mum. "See you later. We're meeting Gran at three."

Dirty Bertie

Dad rolled his eyes. A whole hour in a toy department with Bertie – this was going to be torture!

Dibbles' toy department was on the fourth floor. Bertie's eyes lit up as they stepped out of the lift. It was an Aladdin's cave of wonders: board games, scooters, skateboards, super gunge shooters and gadgets galore.

Bertie picked up a pirate cutlass and swished it through the air. "AHARRRR!" he roared.

"Put that down!" hissed Dad. "You'll break something!"

"May I be of any help, sir?"

A tall, silver-haired shop assistant loomed over them.

"It's okay, thanks, we're just looking," said Dad, grabbing Bertie's sword.

Dirty Bertie

"Anything special?" asked the assistant. "We have a brand new range of trampolines."

"Maybe a bit dangerous – and expensive," said Dad.

"But we're loaded!" said Bertie. "We've just won the lottery."

"Ha ha! We can all dream, can't we?" laughed the shop assistant.

"It's not a dream, it's true!" said Bertie. "We're rich!"

Suddenly they had the assistant's full attention. "Well, I *do* apologize, sir," he said. "In that case, may I show you our luxury toys over here."

Bertie gazed at the toy spaceships and gamma-ray guns. Then something else caught his eye – a gleaming red sports car, just his size.

Dirty Bertie

"Look at this, Dad!" he cried.

"Ah yes, our junior Ferrari," said the shop assistant. "It has a rechargeable battery, working headlights and a top speed of ten miles an hour."

"WOW!" said Bertie. Imagine arriving at school in his own Ferrari! Even Royston Rich hadn't got one of those.

"Can I get in?" asked Bertie, eagerly.

"By all means," said the shop assistant.

Bertie climbed into the driving seat.

Dirty Bertie

"How much does it cost?" asked Dad, anxiously.

The assistant showed him the price tag. Dad turned pale. It was more than he'd paid for their family car.

"VROOM! VROOM!" cried Bertie, imagining he was on the Formula One starting grid. The dashboard had lots of lights, switches and buttons. Bertie pointed to a silver key.

"What's this for?" he asked.

"Don't touch that!" cried the shop assistant.

VROOOOOM!

The car's engine roared into life. Bertie's foot was on the accelerator and the Ferrari took off like a rocket.

"WOAH!" squawked Bertie, gripping the steering wheel. "I CAN'T STOP!"

Dirty Bertie

Customers dived out of the way as the Ferrari zoomed straight for them. Bertie turned the wheel and screeched round a corner.

"BRAKE!" yelled Dad. "USE THE BRAKE…!"

Dirty Bertie

"WHICH ONE?" wailed Bertie.

CRASH!

Too late, Bertie ploughed into a display cabinet of dolls, sending them flying in the air. Dad groaned and buried his face in his hands. He knew he should never have agreed to take Bertie shopping.

CHAPTER 4

At three o'clock, Dad and Bertie took the lift to the tea rooms. Mum and Suzy were already there, surrounded by shopping bags.

Dad rolled his eyes. "I thought you were just looking at shoes?" he said.

"We bought shoes," said Mum. "Plus one or two other things we needed.

Dirty Bertie

Anyway, how did you and Bertie get on?"

"Don't ask," sighed Dad. They'd been made to pay for all the damage Bertie had caused, which had cost a small fortune.

Dad slumped into a chair. "Let's just say it's a good job that Gran's won the lottery," he said.

"Here she comes now," said Suzy.

Gran kissed them all and took a seat.

"This *is* a surprise," she said. "Tea at Dibbles, how nice!"

Mum smiled. "Order anything you like," she said. "It's our treat."

"Really? *Anything?*" said Bertie. He'd been eyeing the cakes and had decided to try them all.

The waiter came over. Mum ordered sandwiches, the special cake selection and champagne for the adults. She turned to Gran.

"Well!" she said. "Tell us all the details."

"How much did we win?" asked Bertie. "A million? Ten million?"

Gran blinked at them, confused. "But I explained on the phone. Didn't Bertie tell you?" she said.

"Tell us what?" said Dad.

Dirty Bertie

"I won twenty pounds," said Gran.

There was a long stony silence.

"Twenty pounds?" cried Mum. "But Bertie said you'd won the lottery!"

"I won a prize, yes. I didn't win the lottery," said Gran. "I told you, Bertie, weren't you listening?"

Everyone turned to glare at Bertie.

He slid down slowly in his seat. Oops! He remembered dropping the phone and rushing off before Gran had finished speaking. It turned out they wouldn't be getting a swimming pool, servants or a Ferrari, after all.

"BERTIE!" groaned Mum.

"We should have known," said Suzy.

Dad had gone very pale. "Do you know how much today has cost us?" he said.

Just then the waiter appeared.

Dirty Bertie

"Your cakes and champagne, madam."
Bertie grabbed an iced bun and
crammed it into his mouth. He had a
feeling there might not be any more
treats for quite a while.

CHAPTER 1

Miss Boot stood at the front of class.

"Good morning, children," she said. "As you can see, we have a visitor with us today."

Bertie sat up. It was Mrs Nicely, his next door neighbour! What on earth was *she* doing in his class?

"Mrs Nicely has kindly offered to teach

a cookery class," said Miss Boot.

Mrs Nicely smiled. "Who would like to learn how to bake a cake?"

A cake? Bertie loved cakes! Mainly he liked eating them, but he was willing to have a go at making one. At home his parents didn't even let him make toast in case he burned the house down. But if he made a cake he could scoff it all himself! YUM!

"As you know, it's Mrs Fossil's last day and the staff are planning a little party for her," said Miss Boot. "What could be nicer than a special cake made by one of you?"

Bertie's face fell. No way was Mrs Fossil getting her greedy hands on *his* cake. Mrs Fossil was about a hundred years old and had been teaching at the

Dirty Bertie

school since the Stone Age. Today she was finally retiring. About time, too, in Bertie's opinion – he wished Miss Boot would hurry up and retire as well.

Later that morning, Bertie's class gathered in the school kitchen with Mrs Nicely.

"Now children," she said, "who can tell me what we need to make a cake?"

Amanda Fibb's hand shot up.

"Eggs," she said.

"Self-raising flour," said Know-All Nick.

"Chocolate buttons," said Bertie.

Mrs Nicely frowned. "Chocolate buttons are not essential."

"They are if it's a chocolate button cake," argued Bertie.

Mrs Nicely silently counted to ten. When she'd agreed to teach a cookery class, no one had warned her it would be with Bertie's class. The boy was a walking nightmare and his manners were appalling.

"Please leave your nose alone, Bertie," she sighed. "Now, we are going to make a simple sponge cake. Once it's baked,

40

you can decorate it any way you like."

Bertie eyed the jars of cake decorations greedily. There were sprinkles, stars, silver balls, chocolate buttons and chocolate shavings. His cake would definitely need all of them.

Mrs Nicely showed them how to make a cake mix by weighing out the ingredients. Then she put them into pairs to have a go. Luckily Bertie got paired with Darren. He read the recipe.

"What's 300g of sugar?" Bertie asked.

"Don't ask me," said Darren. "Don't we have to weigh it?"

"That'll take forever," said Bertie. "It's quicker to just tip it all in."

He poured in the whole jar and added the butter. Next came the flour and the eggs.

Darren inspected the sloppy yellow mixture.

"Is it meant to have bits of eggshell?" he asked.

Bertie sighed – some people were so fussy! He tried to fish out the bits with his fingers but they were too slippery. What did it matter? A few bits of eggshell would add a nice crunch.

"What's next?" Bertie asked.

"Beat well until mixed," Darren read out. Bertie grabbed the wooden spoon and attacked the bowl.

THWACK! BASH! SPLAT!

"Not so hard, Bertie!" cried Mrs Nicely. "You're slopping it everywhere!"

"Sorry," mumbled Bertie. "Darren said to beat it up."

Once it was done, Darren poured the mixture into a cake tin, ready for the oven. He checked the recipe.

"Hang on," he said. "We missed out the pinch of salt." He reached for the salt jar but found it empty. "Where's it all gone?" he asked.

"That's not salt, it's sugar," said Bertie.

"No, it's not, you dummy! Look at the label!" cried Darren.

Dirty Bertie

Bertie's mouth fell open. He had put a ton of salt in their cake mix!

"The recipe says a pinch, not the whole jar!" said Darren.

Bertie shrugged. How was he meant to know? Sugar and salt looked exactly the same.

"Calm down, it'll be all right," he said.

"All right?" moaned Darren. "Cakes are meant to be sweet. Ours will taste like a bag of crisps!"

CHAPTER 2

Bertie and Darren inspected their sponge cake, which was cooling off after baking.

"Looks okay to me," said Bertie, poking it with a finger.

Darren pulled a face. "Well I'm not eating it," he said. "It'll taste of salt."

"Once we decorate it who's going to know?" asked Bertie.

Dirty Bertie

"Anyone who tastes it," replied Darren.

"But they won't," said Bertie. "It's *our* cake and no one's going to touch it. At least they won't want it for Mrs Fossil's party."

Mrs Nicely clapped her hands for silence.

"Right, children, now for my favourite part," she said. "You can ice your cake with any flavour you like and then add the decorations. Remember, I will be judging the cakes and the best one will be presented to Mrs Fossil."

Bertie snorted. Luckily their cake didn't stand a chance. On the next table, Know-All Nick and Amanda Fibb were decorating a perfect golden sponge. It had lemon icing and tiny sugar flowers. *Trust smarty pants Nick to show off,* thought Bertie.

They set to work decorating their own cake. Darren slopped on thick, gloopy brown icing. Next they added chocolate sprinkles, chocolate buttons, chocolate stars and chocolate shavings.

"There!" said Bertie. "I think it looks pretty good."

"You haven't tasted it," said Darren glumly.

Dirty Bertie

The cakes were laid out on a long
table for Mrs Nicely to judge. She
moved down the line until she reached
a brown mud pie, buried under a
gloopy mountain of chocolate.

"Good heavens! Who made this
one?" she gasped.

Dirty Bertie

Bertie raised his hand. "Me and Darren."

"I might have known," sighed Mrs Nicely. "Well, it's very, er … big."

She hurried on to the other cakes.

Dirty Bertie

"I must say that *some* of these cakes look delicious," she said. "But one stands out from the rest. Who made this luscious lemon cake?"

Amanda Fibb and Know-All Nick stepped forward, beaming proudly.

"Wonderful!" said Mrs Nicely. "Perfectly baked and I love the little sugar flowers. Mrs Fossil will be delighted."

Dirty Bertie

HUH! thought Bertie. Who wanted to eat Nick's drippy old lemon cake? It didn't even have any chocolate! Mrs Fossil was welcome to it.

The bell rang for break time.

"Now, children, always leave the kitchen tidy," said Mrs Nicely. "Bertie and Darren, you can stay behind to clear the tables."

Bertie rolled his eyes. Why did he always get picked for the rotten jobs?

"Can't we go now?" grumbled Bertie after five minutes. "We're missing break."

"One more thing," said Mrs Nicely. "Move all these cakes on to the side so they can be collected at home time."

She hurried off to the staff room.

"What about our cake?" said Bertie.

Dirty Bertie

"You take it home, I don't want it," said Darren.

"I bet Whiffer will eat it, he eats anything," sighed Bertie. It seemed a terrible waste.

The cake was dripping chocolate on to the worktop.

Bertie frowned. "It's starting to melt."

"Stick it in the fridge," suggested Darren, "or we'll have to wipe the tables again."

Bertie opened the fridge, which was packed full. On the top shelf sat Nick's luscious lemon cake that Mrs Nicely had set aside for the party. Bertie took it out, and replaced it with their chocolate blob cake.

"What are you doing?" asked Darren.

"Making room for ours," said Bertie.

Dirty Bertie

"But that's Nick's cake for the party!"

"So?" said Bertie. "It can go over there with the— Ooops!"

He accidentally tilted the plate and the cake slid off, hitting the floor.

SPLAT!

Bertie and Darren stared in horror.

"Now look what you've done!" cried Darren.

Bertie tried to scrape the lemon cake back on to the plate. It didn't look quite as luscious as before. The sugar flowers were smashed and half of the icing remained stuck to the floor.

"What are we going to do?" groaned Bertie.

"Don't ask me, *you* dropped it!" said Darren.

Bertie looked around in a panic. Mrs Nicely would go bonkers. He opened the nearest cupboard and hid the lemon cake behind some saucepans.

"Come on!" he said. "Let's get out of here!"

CHAPTER 3

Back in class, Bertie and Darren didn't mention their little accident. They didn't even tell Eugene in case anyone overheard. Mrs Fossil's farewell party was taking place in the staff room at lunchtime. Bertie pictured the moment when they came to present the cake and found it gone. At least no one could pin

Dirty Bertie

the blame on him.

DRRRRING! The lunch bell rang. The class hurried out, but Bertie and his friends weren't fast enough.

"Bertie, Darren!" boomed Miss Boot. "I have a little job for you. And you, too, Eugene."

"But Miss, it's lunchtime!" moaned Bertie.

"This won't take long," said Miss Boot. "I need two children to serve sandwiches at the party."

Dirty Bertie

Normally she would have chosen two sensible children but they'd all run off.

Bertie groaned. "Do we *have* to?"

"Splendid, I knew I could rely on you," said Miss Boot. "Run down to the staff room and I'll join you in a minute. Not you, Eugene."

Bertie and Darren trailed off. This was turning into one of those days.

"Now, Eugene," said Miss Boot. "I want you to fetch the party cake from the fridge in the kitchen. It's a surprise, so don't let Mrs Fossil see it."

Eugene nodded. At least he didn't have to stand around serving food like a waiter. He hurried off to the kitchen. The fridge stood in the corner. On the top shelf he found a cake – but not the one he was expecting. Hadn't

Dirty Bertie

Mrs Nicely picked Nick's luscious lemon cake for the party? Eugene asked a dinner lady.

"'Scuse me… Miss Boot sent me to fetch a cake?" he said.

Dirty Bertie

"That's right, it's in the fridge," said the dinner lady.

"You mean this one?"

"Must be, if it's in there," said the dinner lady.

Eugene shrugged. Miss Boot must know what she was doing – although the cake looked exactly like Bertie and Darren's chocolate blob cake.

Five minutes later Eugene knocked at the staff room door.

Miss Skinner, the Head, answered. "Yes?"

"I brought the cake," said Eugene.

Miss Skinner stared. "Is that it? Good grief! You'd better put it on the table."

Eugene set the cake down where he was told. He hoped Mrs Fossil liked chocolate, because there was plenty of it.

CHAPTER 4

Bertie glanced at the clock – he was starving! Mrs Nicely was watching him like a hawk while she made the tea. So far, all he'd managed to steal was one measly cucumber sandwich from the plate. How long did they have to stand here? Mrs Fossil's party was as dull as a Monday morning. There were no games, sweets or prizes – just teachers standing around yakking and drinking tea.

Darren appeared at Bertie's side.

"We're done for," he muttered. "I've just seen the cake they're giving her."

"So?" said Bertie.

"It's *our* chocolate cake!" said Darren.

Bertie gaped. "What? It can't be!"

"IT IS!" said Darren. "See for yourself. They must have got the wrong one."

"But I left our cake in the fridge," said Bertie.

"Exactly," said Darren. "That's where the party cake was until you dropped it!"

Bertie turned pale. This was a disaster! He'd hoped they'd choose another cake to replace Nick's lemon cake, but not *theirs*. Anything but that.

"It's got salt in it!" hissed Bertie.

"You're telling me – a whole jar!" said Darren. "They'll be sick as dogs!"

Bertie was starting to feel a bit sick himself.

"Where is it? We've got to do something!" he whispered.

Darren pointed to the table across the room. Bertie pushed his way through the crowd towards it. But just then Miss Skinner clapped her hands…

"Thank you all for coming," she said. "I just want to say how much we're all going to miss dear Mrs Fossil. She has taught at this school for twenty-five years…"

Bertie reached the table. If he could just hide the chocolate cake they were saved.

Dirty Bertie

"…And so," said Miss Skinner, "we'd like to present you with a little something the children have made. Bertie, would you bring the cake, please?"

Bertie gulped. "M-me?"

"Yes, hurry up."

Dirty Bertie

Bertie turned pale. Everyone in the room was waiting for him! There was no escape. He carried the cake over to Miss Skinner as if it was a ticking time-bomb. Mrs Fossil's face fell when she saw the blobby mess on the plate.

"Oh," she said. "It's very … um … brown, isn't it?"

"Yes, but I'm sure it tastes delicious," said Miss Skinner. "Let me cut everyone a piece."

Bertie watched in horror as Miss Skinner cut thick slices of cake and handed them round to all the teachers.

Darren edged towards the door. Bertie stood frozen to the spot as Mrs Fossil bit into her slice of cake. She chewed for a moment. Her face turned purple. She clutched at her throat.

"URRRGH!" she croaked. "WATER!"

"I beg your pardon?" said Miss Skinner.

"It's SALTY!" gasped Mrs Fossil. "Are you trying to *poison* me?"

Around the room, teachers were gulping and gasping and

looking as if they might be sick on their plates.

Miss Skinner tried the cake and immediately spat it out.

"*Eugh!* What *is* this?" she cried. "Mrs Nicely, which child made this cake?"

Mrs Nicely had gone red. "But this is the wrong cake!" she said. "It's not the one I chose at all. This is *Bertie's* chocolate cake!"

"BERTIE?" boomed Miss Boot.

"BERTIE!" roared Miss Skinner.

They both turned in time to see Bertie trying to sneak out of the door.

Miss Boot beckoned him over with a long finger.

"BERTIE! Come here!" she smiled. "I've got a lovely chocolate cake that needs finishing…"

DEMON DOLLY

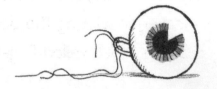

CHAPTER 1

Bertie thumped upstairs. He was playing Hide and Seek. Darren was also hiding while Eugene was 'it'.

Where to hide? The bathroom? His bedroom? Wait, Suzy's room, of course! That was the last place Eugene would look. Bertie sneaked in, closing the door.

"Coming, ready or not!" yelled Eugene.

Dirty Bertie

Quick, under the bed, thought Bertie. He dashed over…

CRUNCH!

Bertie looked down. Yikes! He'd trodden on Molly Dolly!

Suzy had had Molly Dolly since she was four. She was her favourite doll – the only one Suzy refused to part with. Bertie picked her up. Her head lolled to one side then fell off. No!

Bertie tried to jam it back on. One of the blue eyes popped out and rolled under the bed.

Help! Suzy would go bananas when she found out. Bertie wasn't allowed in her room on pain

Dirty Bertie

of death. He wrestled with the doll's head, but it was hopeless. He'd really done it this time.

BLAM! The door burst open.

"FOUND YOU!" cried Eugene triumphantly. "I got Darren, too."

"Only because I sneezed," said Darren, trailing in. "What's that?"

Bertie held up the headless doll. "It's Suzy's. I sort of trod on it," he groaned.

Darren shrugged. "So what? It's only a stupid doll."

"Not to Suzy," said Bertie. "It's Molly Dolly. Gran gave it to her and she goes mad if anyone even touches it."

"She's lost her head," Eugene pointed out.

"I know that," sighed Bertie. "And I can't get it back on."

They took it in turns to try and fix Molly's head. Darren bashed it with his fist, but that didn't work either. Bertie sank down on the bed in despair.

"Glue," said Eugene. "Where do you keep the glue?"

They found some glue in the kitchen and set to work. Pretty soon most of the glue was on Molly's face and hair. But it hadn't helped. Molly's head was

Dirty Bertie

stuck on, but it lolled
to one side. With
one eye missing,
she looked like
something out of a
horror film.

Darren grinned.
"If you ask me it's
a big improvement,"
he said.

"It's not funny!" moaned Bertie.

Suzy would guess who'd done it
right away. Her scream would be heard
halfway down the road. She'd tell Mum
and Dad, and they'd make him pay for
a new doll out of his pocket money.
Unless… Bertie suddenly saw a way
out. It was tough on Molly, but she *was*
only a doll…

"We've got to get rid of her," he said. "If Suzy can't find Molly, she won't know what happened."

"She'll blame you anyway," Darren argued.

"Maybe, but she won't be able to prove anything," said Bertie. "I'll say I never touched her doll."

He looked around for somewhere to hide Molly. Suzy was at Bella's house, but she'd be back soon. He had to act fast. The minute Suzy noticed Molly was missing she'd search every room in the house. Bertie broke into a smile. Molly wouldn't *be* in the house – she'd be somewhere no one would find her. He hurried downstairs and went outside to the dustbins. Opening the brown bin, he dangled Molly by one leg.

"Ah! Poor thing!" sighed Eugene.

PLOP! Bertie dropped Molly into
the rubbish, pushing her down under
the soggy layers of potato peel and tea
bags.

"Bye-bye, Molly," he said, closing the
lid. "Don't lose your head!"

CHAPTER 2

"Do-do-doo, do-do-doo!"

Bertie always sang to himself when cleaning his teeth before bedtime. Mainly because he knew it drove his sister mad.

Suzy poked her head round the door. "Have you been in my room?" she demanded.

Bertie stopped singing.

Dirty Bertie

"WHAT?" he said.

"My room — have you been nosing around?" repeated Suzy.

"Why would I go in your stinky old room?" asked Bertie.

"I can't find Molly Dolly," said Suzy. "She was there when I went to school."

Bertie gulped, swallowing a mouthful of toothpaste. He'd forgotten about the doll. Still, he was safe — he'd disposed of the evidence.

"*Well*, have you seen her?" asked Suzy, glaring.

"Seen who?"

"Molly Dolly!" snapped Suzy.

"No!" said Bertie. "I haven't touched your dopey doll."

"Well, someone has. Did one of your smelly friends go in my room?" said Suzy.

Dirty Bertie

"No! I told you!" cried Bertie.

"Hmm." Suzy narrowed her eyes. "If you're lying, you are in *big* trouble," she warned.

Bertie leaned against the wall and breathed a sigh of relief. He'd got away with it. Suzy couldn't prove a thing. In a couple of days the bin men would collect the rubbish and Molly Dolly would be history.

Back in her bedroom, Suzy searched her room again. She could have sworn that Molly was there earlier. Maybe she'd fallen under the bed? She got down on her hands and knees to look. No Molly – but something small and shiny caught her eye. She reached a

hand under the bed. A tiny blue glass
eye stared back at her.

Molly Dolly had blue eyes! Suzy
frowned. Someone had been in here and
no prizes for guessing who — her bogey-
nosed little brother. But if this was Molly's
eye, where was the rest of her?

Suzy had a terrible thought. She
rushed downstairs and hurried outside.
She opened the brown bin.

"NOOOO!"

Poor Molly Dolly lay buried under
tea bags and potato peel. As Suzy

79

picked her up, Molly's head came off in
her hand. Her face was sticky and she
squinted from one eye.

"You wait, Bertie!" said Suzy. She'd
pay him back for this. She'd put a
worm in his lunch box; she'd leave a
slug in his bed… But would that bother
Bertie? No! He loved worms, slugs and
disgusting things!

Suzy stroked Molly's sticky hair. Hang
on… Bertie thought the doll was gone
forever – well, he was in for a shock.
Molly Dolly was
about to rise
from the dead!

CHAPTER 3

It was almost midnight. Bertie lay in bed, fast asleep.

BOO-HOO-HOO!

His eyes blinked open. What was that? Had he been dreaming? He was sure that he heard crying.

BOO-HOO-HOO!

There it was again – a faint sobbing

coming from somewhere outside his room. Maybe Whiffer had escaped from the kitchen and got upstairs? But it didn't sound like Whiffer. He'd be scratching at the door and whining to be let in, or jumping on the bed. Bertie sat up and listened.

"WUH-HUH-HUH!"

It sounded like a baby crying! The hairs prickled on the back of Bertie's neck. There were no babies in the house, were there? When his parents had tried to sell the house Bertie had told visitors that it was haunted. But surely he'd made that up...

CREEEEEAK!

What was that? Bertie pulled the duvet higher. There was something out on the landing!

Dirty Bertie

"H-hello?" he croaked. "Who's there?"

Silence.

Suddenly a face rose into view: a tiny, pale face with wild hair and one staring eye…

"BERTIE!" the doll hissed. "It's me!"

"ARRRRRGH!"

Dirty Bertie

Bertie dived under his covers and lay there breathing hard. No, it wasn't possible! Molly Dolly was gone and buried in the dustbin. Besides, she was a doll – she couldn't move or speak … not unless she was … A GHOST!

Bertie shivered. He peeped his head slowly above the duvet. Phew – it had gone! He flopped back on his pillow, his heart beating fast. This was his own fault. He'd dumped poor Molly in the dustbin. Now her ghost had returned to haunt him!

Back in her room, Suzy smiled to herself. Her plan had worked like a dream. With a little sticky tape she'd managed to attach Molly's head back on. Bertie had practically jumped out of his skin when the doll rose up and spoke like a ghost. She wished she could have seen his terrified face. But she wasn't finished yet – the haunting had only just begun. Suzy tied Molly to a stick and carefully poked her out of the window. Bertie's bedroom was just next door.

Bertie tossed and turned, trying to get to sleep. *There are no ghosts,* he told himself. It was just his imagination playing tricks. In the morning he'd laugh about this – fancy thinking that a ghost dolly was haunting him! Ha ha! It was the most stupid idea in—

TAP, TAP, TAP!

Dirty Bertie

Hold on, what was that noise?

TAP, TAP, TAP!

Something was tapping at his window. Bertie kept his eyes shut tight, too scared to look. It was no use, he had to see what it was. Slowly he turned his head and peeped…

ARRGH! There it was at the window! The same staring face with one eye. Molly Dolly was trying to get in!

Dirty Bertie

"WAAAAH!"

Bertie dived out of bed and bolted along to his parents' room.

"HELP! SAVE ME!" he gasped, barging in.

Dad moaned. Mum sat up in bed.

"Bertie, what on earth's the matter?" she said.

"IT'S AFTER ME!" wailed Bertie. "DON'T LET IT GET ME!"

"What is? What are you talking about?" said Mum.

"MOLLY DOLLY!" cried Bertie. "She's a ... a ghost!"

Mum rubbed her eyes wearily.

"It's one o'clock in the morning," she groaned. "You just had a nightmare."

"I didn't!" cried Bertie. "It was at the window – I saw it!"

Dirty Bertie

Mum got out of bed and threw on her dressing gown. She took Bertie back to his room.

"Where? Where's this ghost?" she demanded.

"It was right there – at the window. I saw it!" answered Bertie.

Mum rolled her eyes. "There's nothing there!" she said. "You just had a bad dream. Now *please* can we all get some sleep?"

CHAPTER 4

Bertie stared at his alarm clock. It was a quarter to two. He wished morning would come. Every time he closed his eyes, the wind moaned or a floorboard creaked and he thought it was the ghost. If he ever survived this, he swore he'd never set foot in Suzy's bedroom again. Maybe Molly Dolly would leave him alone if he promised to be good?

In the next bedroom, Suzy had one last trick to play — something that would scare the pants off her horrible little brother. She rummaged through her cupboard until she found what she wanted — Kutie Kitty. It was years since she'd played with the toy kitten. She hoped that the battery still worked.

Dirty Bertie

Bertie's eyes snapped open. What was that? *Keep calm, it's only the wind,* he told himself. He should have shut the door when he came back to bed. Perhaps he should get up now and close it…

WHIRR! CLICK, CLICK!

Bertie's blood ran cold. Nooo! It was back. The one-eyed ghost. It was out on the landing. If he got out of bed maybe he could slam the door in its face. But that wouldn't work – ghosts could walk *through* doors!

WHIRR! CLICK, CLICK!

Bertie shrank down under his covers. *Please, please, don't let it get me!* he prayed.

Suddenly a strange creature appeared

in the doorway. Argh! There it was! The ghost of Molly – and it was walking! It had grown four legs and a furry white body!

WHIRR! CLICK, CLICK! WHIRR!

The ghost doll plodded closer, twitching its head.

Dirty Bertie

"ARRRRRRGHHHH!"

Bertie's yell was loud enough to wake the whole house. He shot out of bed, leaped over the doll and scrambled out of the door.

Seconds later, he dived on to his parents' bed.

"MU-UUM! HEEELP!"

"BERTIE!" groaned Mum.

"Not again," moaned Dad.

"IT'S AFTER ME!" babbled Bertie. "Don't let it get me."

"Bertie, how many times…? There's nothing there," said Mum.

"There is! It's got four furry legs and one eye," wailed Bertie.

Mum jumped out of bed. She couldn't take much more of this. She dragged Bertie back to his room and snapped on the light.

"LOOK!" she cried. "THERE IS
NOTHING THERE!"

Something lay on the floor, whirring
and kicking its legs. Bertie bent down
and picked it up. It was a toy kitten –
with Molly's head.

Bertie stared in disbelief.

"*This* is what you were scared of?"
cried Mum.

Bertie sheepishly nodded his head.
This was Suzy's doing. She must have
found Molly buried in the bin and
planned her revenge. Worse still, he
couldn't tell on her without landing
himself in big trouble.

Mum was frowning. "Hang on,"
she said. "Isn't this Molly Dolly? What
happened to her head?"

Dirty Bertie

Bertie turned red. "Um … is it really that late?" he said, looking at the clock. "I'd better get to bed, I've got school in the morning."

Mum gave him a withering look and stormed back to her room.

Bertie switched off the light and climbed into bed. Peace at last. No more

babies crying or ghosts at the window.
But wait, what was this on his pillow?
Something small and shiny. He switched
on his bedside lamp.

YARGGGHHHH! IT WAS
SOMEBODY'S EYEBALL!